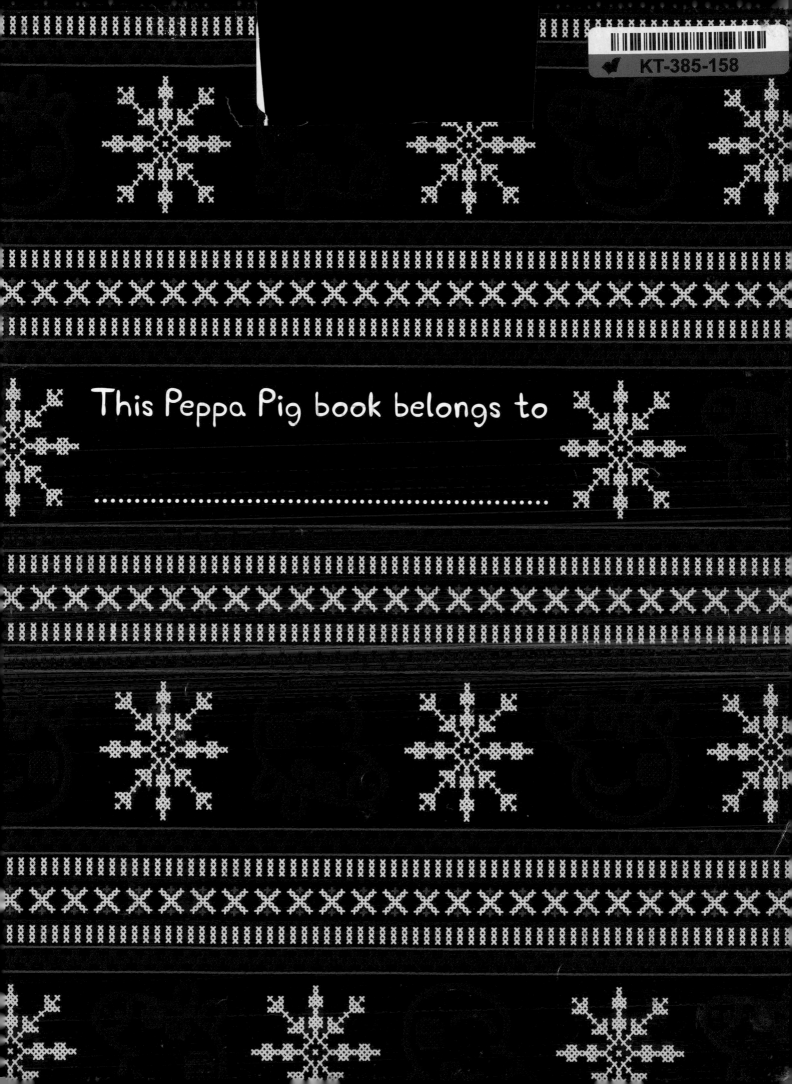

This Peppa Pig book belongs to

....

LADYBIRD BOOKS

UK | USA | Canada | Ireland | Australia
India | New Zealand | South Africa

Ladybird Books is part of the Penguin Random House group of companies
whose addresses can be found at global.penguinrandomhouse.com.
www.penguin.co.uk   www.puffin.co.uk   www.ladybird.co.uk

 Penguin
Random House
UK

First published 2017
001

Printed in China

A CIP catalogue record for this book is available from the British Library
ISBN: 978-0-241-28928-0

All correspondence to:
Ladybird Books, Penguin Random House Children's,
80 Strand, London, WC2R 0RL

Contents

Snort!

Hello, Peppa!

This is Peppa Pig. She lives in a house on a hill with her little brother, George, and her mummy and daddy.

George

Peppa

Cousin Chloe

Daddy Pig

Snort!

Mummy Pig

6

Dot-to-Dot Dinosaur

Join the dots, then colour in this picture of George's toy dinosaur. Can you say the sound it makes?

George's dinosaur says

" Grrrr! "

How loudly can you say "Grrrr!"?

Time to Play!

Peppa and George are having fun playing in their bedroom. Look at the five objects at the bottom of the page. Can you spot them all in the big picture?

Where is Peppa's teddy?

What colour is George's top?

What can you see through the window?

How many building blocks can you count?

Tick the boxes when you find each of these objects in the big picture.

Answers: Peppa's teddy is on the bed, George's top is blue, you can see the moon through the window, there are seven building blocks.

Story Time

Fruit Day

Peppa and her family are at the supermarket. It's Fruit Day! Look – there's Mr Potato, Mrs Carrot, Sweet Cranberry and Little Sprout!
"Welcome to Fruit Day," says Mr Potato, "where the magic of fruit never ends!"

Mr Potato, Mrs Carrot, Sweet Cranberry and Little Sprout sing their special Fruit Day song . . .

♪ "Apple, orange and banana, 🎵

Pear and pineapple, too!

Eat five pieces of fruit a day

♪ Because they're good for you!"

Peppa's friends are at the supermarket, too.

"Hello, Peppa! We're choosing our favourite fruit!" says Suzy Sheep. "What's yours?"

"I like apples," says Peppa.

"I like oranges," says Suzy.

"I like bananas," says Emily Elephant.

"I like carrots," says Rebecca Rabbit.

"Carrots are not a fruit," says Edmond Elephant. "They are a vegetable!"

Edmond is a bit of a clever clogs.

"What is your favourite fruit, George?" asks Suzy.

George does not know.

"George likes strawberries the best," says Peppa.

"Taw-berry!" cries George. George LOVES strawberries!

"Smoothies! Smoothies! Get your fruit smoothies here!" calls Miss Rabbit. "A smoothie is a drink made from fruit," Miss Rabbit tells Peppa. "Would you like one?"
"Yes, please!" says Peppa. "Can I have a smoothie made with apples?"

KRRRRRRRRRRRRRR!

Delicious!

"You can have LOTS of different fruit in a smoothie," says Miss Rabbit. "All right," says Peppa. "I'll have apples, raspberries, bananas and more apples, please!"
Miss Rabbit puts some apples, raspberries, bananas and more apples in her blender, then whizzes them up into a smoothie.

Mmmmmmmm!

Now everyone wants a fruit smoothie! This time Miss Rabbit whizzes up some raspberries, blueberries, blackberries and gooseberries.

KRRRRRRRRRRRR!

"What would you like in your smoothie, George?" asks Miss Rabbit.

"Taw-berry!" says George.

"George, your smoothie must have LOTS of different fruit in it," says Peppa.

"How about strawberry and banana?" suggests Emily.

"No!" says George.

"Strawberry and gooseberry?" asks Pedro.

"No!"

"Strawberry and pineapple?" asks Suzy.

"No!"

"Strawberry and carrot?" asks Rebecca.

"No!"

Oh dear! George doesn't want to try a different kind of fruit. He only wants strawberries.

"Maybe George would like to try some dinosaur juice!" says Miss Rabbit.

KRRRRRRRRRRRRR!

"There you go," she says. "One dinosaur juice!"
"Hee! Hee! Dine-saw!" George says.
He drinks it all up.

George LOVES dinosaur juice!

Sluurrrp!

Now everyone wants dinosaur juice!
"Oh dear," says Miss Rabbit. "I've forgotten what I put in it!"
"I can tell you what was in it," says Freddy Fox. "I have a very good sense of smell!"
Freddy smells George's empty smoothie glass.

"There's one banana . . .

. . . three, no, four strawberries . . .

. . . five cherries . . .

. . . one peach . . .

. . . half a pineapple . . .

Sniff!

Sniff!

. . . and something else. What is it?"

"A carrot?" asks Rebecca Rabbit.

"Yes!" cries Freddy.

Miss Rabbit whizzes up lots and lots of dinosaur juice for Peppa and her friends.

"Are you all enjoying Fruit Day?" asks Mr Potato.

"Yes!" everyone cries. "We love fruit!"

"And carrots!" adds Rebecca Rabbit. "We love fruit *and* carrots!"

My Favourite Fruit

Peppa and her friends love fruit. Tick which kinds of fruit you like, too.

☐  apple

☐  orange

☐  blackberry

Try some of the fruit you haven't tasted yet. You might find you like it!

☐  pineapple

☐  banana

☐  raspberry

☐  cherry

☐  pear

☐  gooseberry

☐  kiwi fruit

☐  strawberry

☐  blueberry

☐  melon

Can you draw your favourite fruit in this basket?

My favourite fruit is apple!

Super Smoothies

Would you like a smoothie? Ask a grown-up to whizz up one of these super smoothies for you to try.

Very Berry Smoothie

(Serves 2)

- 1 banana, peeled and chopped
- 20 raspberries
- 5 blackberries
- 300ml milk

Put all the ingredients in a blender, then whizz them together. Add a tablespoon of thick natural yoghurt for a super-creamy smoothie.

Strawberry and Banana Smoothie

(Serves 2)

- 15 strawberries
- 1 banana, peeled and chopped
- 1 tablespoon thick natural yoghurt
- 300ml milk

Put all the ingredients in a blender, then whizz them together. Add more or less milk depending on how thick you like your smoothie.

Dine-saw Green Smoothie

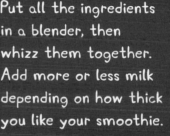

(Serves 2)

- a big handful of fresh baby spinach leaves
- 1 apple, peeled, cored and diced
- 1 slice (around 150g) honeydew melon, peeled and chopped, with seeds removed
- 250ml apple juice

Put all the ingredients in a blender, then whizz them together. If you like, you can add a few green grapes, too!

Peppa's Presents

c b s f

Do you know what these Christmas presents are? Choose the right letters to finish off the words below and find out!

1

George is giving Peppa a _ook about a fairy!

2

Peppa is giving George a _ootball.

3

Mummy and Daddy Pig are giving Peppa a fancy-dress _rown.

4

Peppa is giving Mummy and Daddy Pig some woolly _ocks.

Answers: 1. b – book, 2. f – football, 3. c – crown, 4. s – socks

Up, Up and Away!

Look! Peppa and her family are off for a ride in a hot-air balloon. Colour in the beautiful balloons.

Can you put these balloons in order of size? Number them from 1 to 3, starting with the smallest and ending with the biggest.

Answers: 1. Zoe Zebra's monkey balloon. 2. Suzy Sheep's carrot balloon. 3. George's dinosaur balloon.

23

Royal Tea Party

Candy Cat and Rebecca Rabbit have come to play princesses with Peppa. Can you spot six differences between the two pictures of their princess tea party?

A

Colour in a fairy cake each time you spot a difference.

1

2

3

Peppa loves jelly! Can you make all these wibbly wobbly jellies different flavours with your colouring pencils?

B

4

5

6

Answers: 1. Candy Cat has changed to Suzy Sheep, 2. the cherry is missing from the top of the jelly on the left, 3. Peppa's throne cushion has changed to red, 4. the cupcakes on the right have become a jelly, 5. the carrot cake has become sandwiches, 6. the strawberry cake has become a carrot cake.

25

Princess Peppa

Colour in this picture of Peppa dressed up as a princess. What colour will you choose for her dress?

Match the Tea Sets

Draw lines to help Peppa match up all these pretty teacups and teapots.

1

2

3

4

a

b

c

d

Astronaut George

Look! George is dressed up as an astronaut today.
Can you help him colour in this picture of
a rocket zooming to the moon?

How many stars
of each colour can
you count?

orange   red   blue   yellow   white

Answers: 1 orange star, 2 red stars, 3 blue stars, 4 yellow stars, 5 white stars.

Zoom to the Moon

Say the word "rocket" each time you see the picture of the rocket in this poem.

Look at the little .

Hear its engines roar!

The countdown has begun,

Eight, Seven, Six, Five, Four . . .

Three, Two, One . . . BLAST OFF!

It's zooming to the moon.

Good luck, little .

Come back and see us soon!

George loves dressing up, just like Peppa. Can you match the words to George's costumes?

a dinosaur

b pirate

c robot

Follow the lines with your finger to read the story about how Peppa learns to ice skate.

Peppa

START

Peppa is going ice skating. She has never been skating before.

Oh dear. Ice skating is not as easy as it looks!

"Everyone falls over when they are learning to skate," says Daddy Pig.

Mummy Pig show Peppa what to do "Push with your feet and glide, like this . . . See!"

Goes Skating!

BUMP!

Peppa keeps falling on her bottom on the ice.

Write the word "Wheeeeeee!" here.

Wheeeeeeee!

"Skating is too hard!" says Peppa. "I don't want to do it any more."

Peppa keeps trying, and soon she is skating all by herself.

"Skating is so much fun!" says Peppa.

WHEEEEEEE!

Colour in Peppa.

Fun and Games

Finish colouring in these pictures of some of the games Peppa and her friends like to play.

skipping ☐

hopscotch ☐

leapfrog ☐

Put a tick next to each game if you like playing it, too.

hide-and-seek

32

Memory Puzzle

Look at the picture of Peppa and her family flying a kite on a windy day. Cover up the picture, then see if you can answer all the questions below.

1 Who is flying the kite?

2 What colour are Peppa's boots?

3 How many birds are sitting in the trees?

4 Is Daddy Pig wearing his glasses?

Story Time
The Little Boat

Peppa and her family are going on a picnic!
"The picnic spot is on the other side of the river," says Mummy Pig.
"How do we get across?" asks Peppa.
"We call a little boat by ringing this bell," says Daddy Pig.

Look! It's Grampy Rabbit in his little boat.
"Get in, everyone," calls Grampy Rabbit. "I'll row you across the river!"

Oh dear! Grampy Rabbit's boat is too small to fit everyone in.
Daddy Pig has to stay behind with the picnic.
"Don't worry! I'll come straight back for you!" calls Grampy Rabbit.

Grampy Rabbit sings as he rows Peppa,
George and Mummy Pig across the river.

The Wolf family arrives.
"Hello," says Daddy Pig.
"We're having a picnic.
Would you like to join us?"
"Yes, please," say Mr Wolf,
Mrs Wolf and Wendy.

"Ah, more passengers!" says Grampy Pig, rowing back to the shore.
This time only Mrs Wolf and Wendy fit in the little boat. Daddy Pig and
Mr Wolf have to wait with the picnic. They are getting *very* hungry!
Grampy Rabbit sings as he rows Wendy and Mrs Wolf across the river.

Grampy Rabbit rows back again.
"This time *I'll* row the boat across the river!" says Daddy Pig.
"Good idea," says Grampy Rabbit. "I could do with a rest!"

Daddy Pig rows himself and Mr Wolf across the river.
"Hooray! We're here!" says Daddy Pig when they get to the picnic spot.
"But where's the picnic?" asks Peppa.

Daddy Pig rows back across the river to get the picnic but he can't fit in the little boat with Grampy Rabbit and the picnic basket! "Don't worry. I'll be straight back!" calls Grampy Rabbit as he rows away, leaving Daddy Pig on the shore.

Grampy Rabbit arrives at the picnic spot with the picnic. "Would you like some cheese, Grampy Rabbit?" asks Mummy Pig. "I should get back," says Grampy Rabbit, taking a slice. "I do love cheese!" "I love sandwiches," says Wendy.

Mrs Duck arrives with her friends.
"Would you like some cake, Mrs Duck?" asks Peppa.
"Cake is Daddy's favourite thing. Oh no! Where's Daddy?"
"We forgot Daddy!" cries Mummy Pig.

Poor Daddy Pig is all by himself on the other side of the river.
He rings the bell to call Grampy Rabbit and his little boat.

At last Daddy Pig gets to the picnic spot . . . but where's the picnic?
"I saved you some jelly," says Peppa.
George has saved Daddy Pig a strawberry.

"How nice of you," says Daddy Pig. "Is there any cake?"
"No, we gave it to the ducks," says Peppa. "But Mrs Duck has saved you a worm!"
"Ho! Ho! Thank you, Mrs Duck!" says Daddy Pig, and everyone laughs.

Road Maze

Peppa and her family are off on an adventure to Duck Land. Help them to find their way through the road maze so they don't get lost!

How many greedy ducks can you count? Circle the right answer!

1   5   12

Puzzle Pictures

Summertime Fun

Can you work out which jigsaw pieces complete each picture puzzle?

1

2

a

b

c

d

Answers: 1. c, 2. a

Wintertime Fun

45

Granny Pig's Chickens

Peppa and George are staying with Granny and Grandpa Pig. Look at the pictures and word key below, then at the story on the next page. Say the word every time you see one of the pictures in the story.

George

Peppa

Granny Pig

Grandpa Pig

eggs

lettuces

chickens

and are staying with and .

takes and into the garden to see his . Oh no!

The have all gone! Then Granny Pig's come to peck at the ground.

"Those ate my !" says .

and give the some corn to eat.

The next morning there are four inside the coop.

" for breakfast!" says . Yum! Yum!

"These taste good because the ate lots of corn," says .

"The taste good because the ate my !" says .

Everyone laughs.

Hee! Hee! Snort!

47

A Bike Ride

Peppa and her friends love riding their bikes in the park. Look at the pictures and answer the questions.

1 How many bikes can you see?

2 What colour is Edmond's bike?

3 Who is wearing a red dress?

4 How many birds can you spot?

5 Who has black spots on her bike helmet?

48

Make a Noise with

Join Peppa and George's noisy fun by singing the words below to the tune of "Happy Birthday!" and following the instructions!

Jump in puddles – Splish! Splash!
Jump in puddles – Splish! Splash!
Jump in puddles, muddy puddles!
Jump in puddles – Splish! Splash!

Jump up and down as if you're playing in a very muddy muddle.

Pretend to play a very noisy drum.

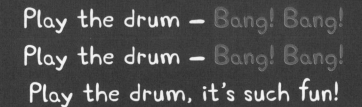

Play the drum – Bang! Bang!
Play the drum – Bang! Bang!
Play the drum, it's such fun!
Play the drum – Bang! Bang!

Peppa and George!

51

Jump up and down the room like a bouncy rabbit!

Jump!

Jump!

Jump!

Be a rabbit – Jump! Jump!
Be a rabbit – Jump! Jump!
Be a rabbit, with fluffy ears!
Be a rabbit – Jump! Jump!

Toot!

Move your arms in circles like the wheels of a train!

Choo! Choo!

Play at trains – Choo! Choo!
Play at trains – Choo! Choo!
Play at trains, toot your horn!
Play at trains – Choo! Choo!

Story Time
Garden Games

It is a lovely sunny day. Peppa, George and Suzy are outside in the garden but they don't know what to play. "We're bored!" Peppa tells Daddy Pig.

Daddy Pig has an idea. He goes inside, then comes back out with an old box of garden games. "Juggling sticks!" cries Suzy. "Watch me juggle!" "Those aren't juggling sticks. They're skittles," says Daddy Pig.

Daddy Pig shows Peppa, Suzy and George how to play skittles.
"We set the skittles up in a row, like this. Then you have to try
to knock them over by rolling this heavy ball."
Peppa goes first. She knocks over two skittles.

Hooray!

Suzy goes next. She knocks over
all the skittles!
"Well done, Suzy!" says Peppa.

Next it's George's turn.
"George can stand closer to the skittles
because he is little," says Daddy Pig.

George tries to throw the ball, but it is too heavy.
"George is too little for skittles," says Peppa.
George begins to cry. He doesn't like being the littlest.

Waaaaaaaa!

"Let's play a different game," says Daddy Pig. "Let's play bat and ball!
We take turns to throw the ball. The person with the bat has to hit the ball
but, if anyone catches it, the person with the bat is out."

Peppa throws the ball to George. George hits the ball, but Suzy catches it. Oh dear. George is out! George begins to cry again. He is too little even for bat and ball.

"You just need a bit more practice, George," says Daddy Pig. "Watch me!" Daddy Pig hits the ball . . .

The ball lands in Mummy Pig's tea! Mummy Pig is not happy. "Please be more careful, Daddy Pig," she says.

Danny Dog arrives. "Can I play bat and ball, too?" asks Danny.
"I think it's time for a different garden game," says Daddy Pig.
"Let's play limbo."

Daddy Pig sets up the limbo pole. "You play music, then you dance
under the pole," he says. "Like this!" Daddy Pig is very good at the limbo!
"Now we put the pole a little bit lower," says Daddy Pig.

Daddy Pig tries again, but his tummy is too big to fit under the pole and he
knocks it off. Everyone else can limbo under the pole, though – even George!

"Let's make the pole even lower," says Daddy Pig.
"That's easy," says Peppa, but she knocks the pole off.
"No one can fit under that!" says Peppa. "It's too low!"
But look! George can do it! George limbo dances under the pole.

"George is the best at limbo dancing because he's little!" says Peppa.
George likes playing garden games! Everyone likes playing garden games!

Whose Hat?

Draw lines to give everyone a hat, or something else to wear on their heads, to match their fancy dress costumes.

1 Danny

2 Peppa

3 George

4 Miss Rabbit

5 Candy

6 Pedro

7 Suzy

58

a crown

b space helmet

c pirate hat

e nurse's hat

d cowboy hat

g firefighter's hat

f knight's helmet

What Comes Next?

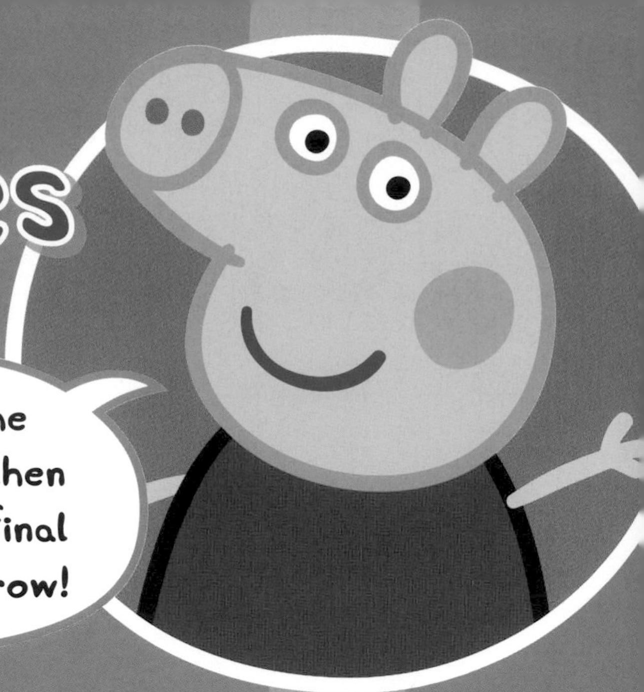

Work out the patterns and then colour in the final shape in each row!

Answers: 1. red heart, 2. yellow star, 3. blue square, 4. white daisy, 5. red boot.

Muddy Puddles

Use the numbers to colour in this picture of Peppa and her family having lots of fun doing their favourite thing — jumping in muddy puddles!

Splish!   Splosh!

Goodbye!

Key 1 2 3 4 5 6 7 8 9 10

61

Look out for these other great Peppa Pig books!

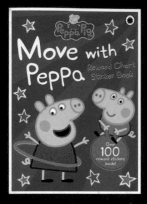

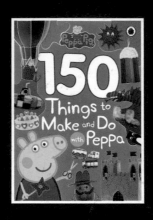

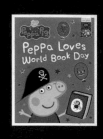

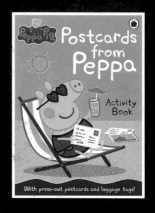

CD and audio download

Buggy Book

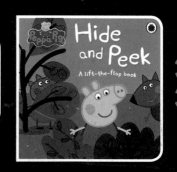

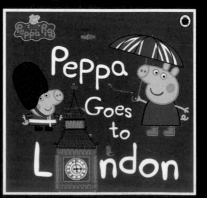